Michelangelo

The Teenage Mutant Ninja Turtles

Splinter, the Sensei

Use the key to find out what day it is.

A	B	C	D	E	F	G	H	I	J	K	L	M	N	O	P	Q	R	S	T	U	V	W	X	Y	Z
26	25	24	23	22	21	20	19	18	17	16	15	14	13	12	11	10	9	8	7	6	5	4	3	2	1

___ ___ ___ ___ ___   ___ ___ ___   ___ ___ ___
14 6   7   26 7   18 12 13   23 26 2

Welcome to the streets of New York City.

The city is filled with adventure—and pizza!

To find out what Raphael thinks of pizza, start at the arrow and, going clockwise around the circle, write the letters in order in the blanks below.

A L G A E T H I S I S B E T T E R T H A N W O R M S A N D

" _____ ____ __ _____

___ ____ _____ ___ _____!"

The Turtles interrupt a crime.

To find out what Raphael thinks of pizza, start at the arrow and, going clockwise around the circle, write the letters in order in the blanks below.

"
_____ _____ _____ _____

_____ _____ _____ _____

_____ _____ _____

_____ _____ _____ _____ _____ !"

ANSWER: "This is better than worms and algae!"

The Turtles interrupt a crime.

The Turtles aren't very good at teamwork.

Michelangelo discovers that the bad guys are really robots with weird alien brains inside!

"Those brain things are all kinds of wrong!" says Michelangelo.

Can you find the brain that is different?

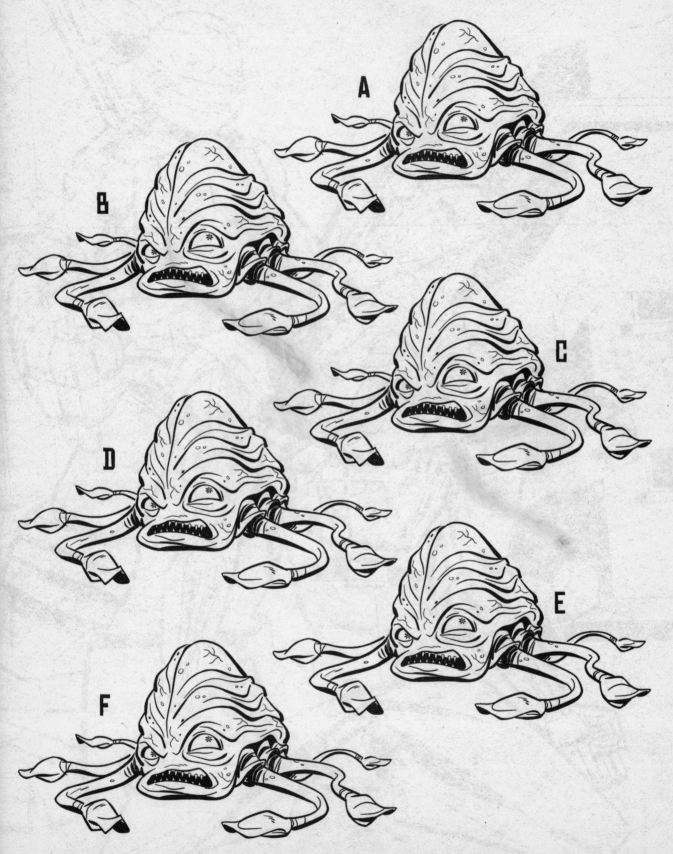

Back in the lair, Splinter says, "Your inability to work together allowed the bad guys to get away."

No one believes Michelangelo's stories about robots and alien brains.

Splinter knows the Turtles need a leader.

To see who he chooses, slowly tilt the page
away from you and read the name.

The Turtles return to the city streets.
"We've got to save that girl," says Leonardo.

"That building has the same logo as the van we're looking for," says Leonardo.

Help the Turtles find the van.

START

FINISH

The Turtles stop the van.
It's filled with the chemical that mutated them!

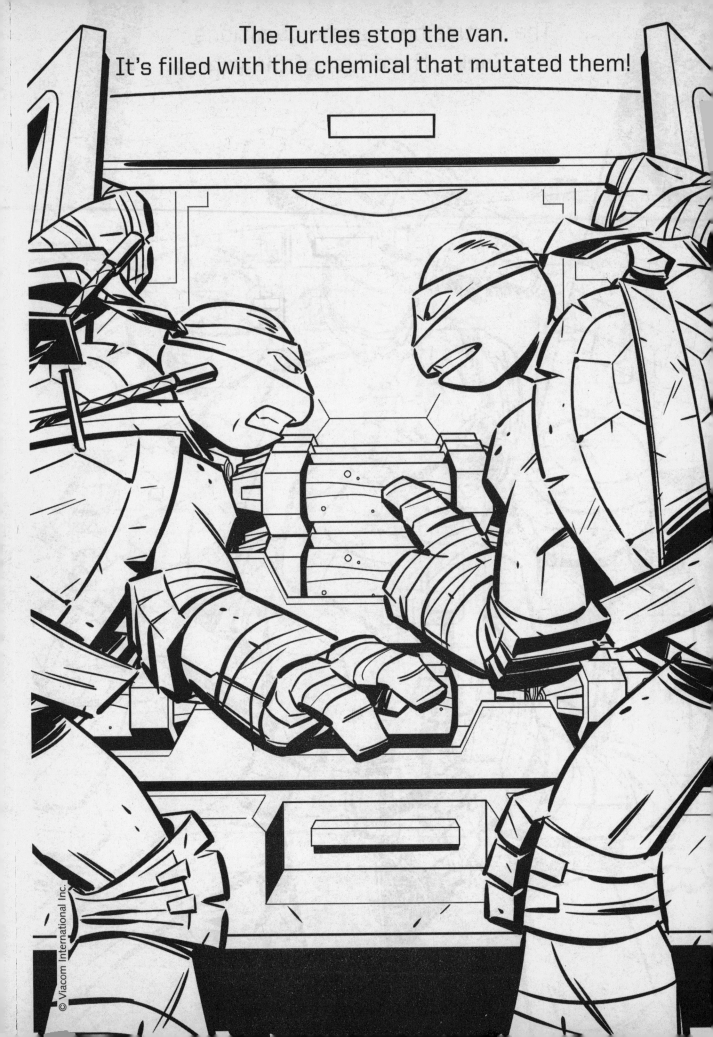

The Turtles have some questions
for Snake, the driver of the van.

Snake tells the Turtles who the bad guys are.
Use the key to learn the name of their evil organization.

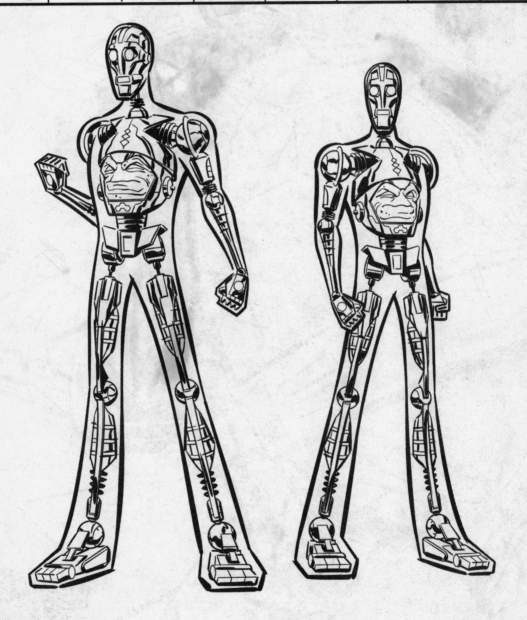

"We should storm the Kraang's factory now!" says Raphael. "It will be an all-you-can-beat buffet!"

"We can't just rush in," says Leonardo.
"We need a plan!"

"We'll go back to the lair and gear up," says Leonardo. "Then we'll use Snake's van to sneak into the Kraang's factory."

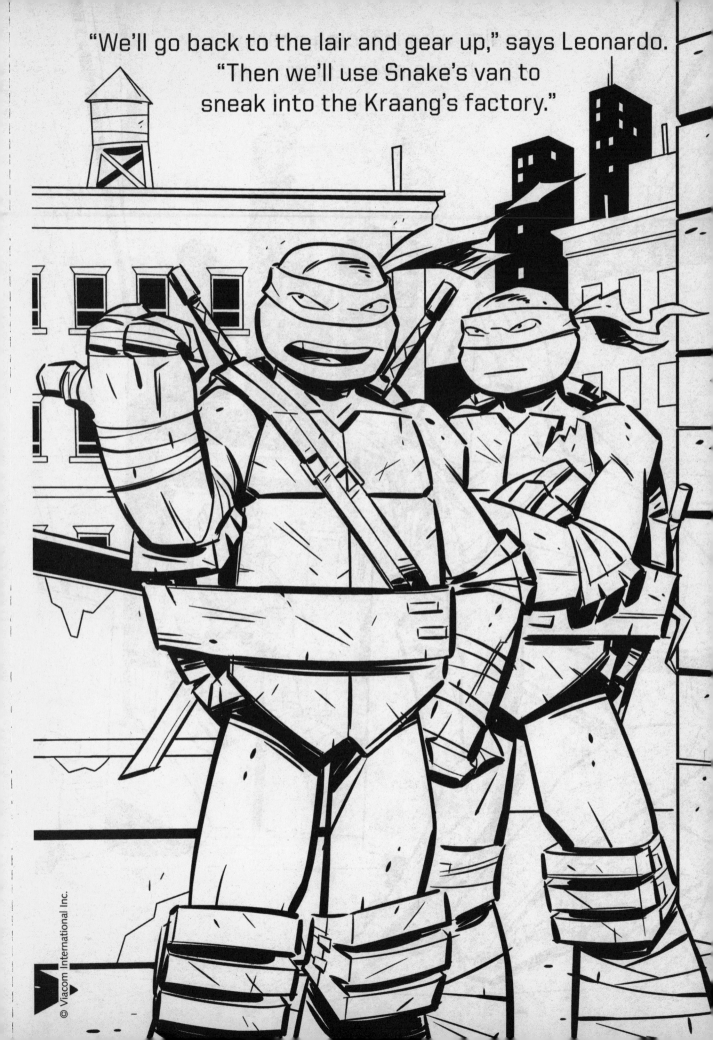

Snake, who is hiding nearby,
hears everything.

That night, a van races toward the Kraang's factory.

Snake has warned the Kraang that the Turtles are coming. They are ready and waiting!

But the Turtles aren't in the van!
They knew Snake was listening and are
sneaking into the Kraang's base another way.

Leonardo and Raphael battle the Kraang—
and make an amazing discovery!

Help Donatello find the girl and her father and lead them to Leonardo.

START

FINISH

ANSWER:

Snake is splashed with the secret chemical—and turns into a giant weed!

"You'd think he would have changed into a snake," Michelangelo says.

The Turtles and the girl, April, escape on a helicopter—but April's father is left behind.

Back at the lair, Splinter tells Leonardo that he is very impressed. "You proved to be an effective leader," he says.

April vows to find her father—and
the Turtles promise to help her!

The Teenage Mutant Ninja Turtles—lean, mean, green, and ready for adventure!

MICHELANGELO!

RAPHAEL!

DONATELLO!

THE TEENAGE MUTANT NINJA TURTLES!

Evil, beware!

N.Y.C.

Michelangelo lets loose!

Donatello gets the job done!

Raphael is right on time!

Leonardo lays down the law!

Ready for battle!

Leonardo leads the way!

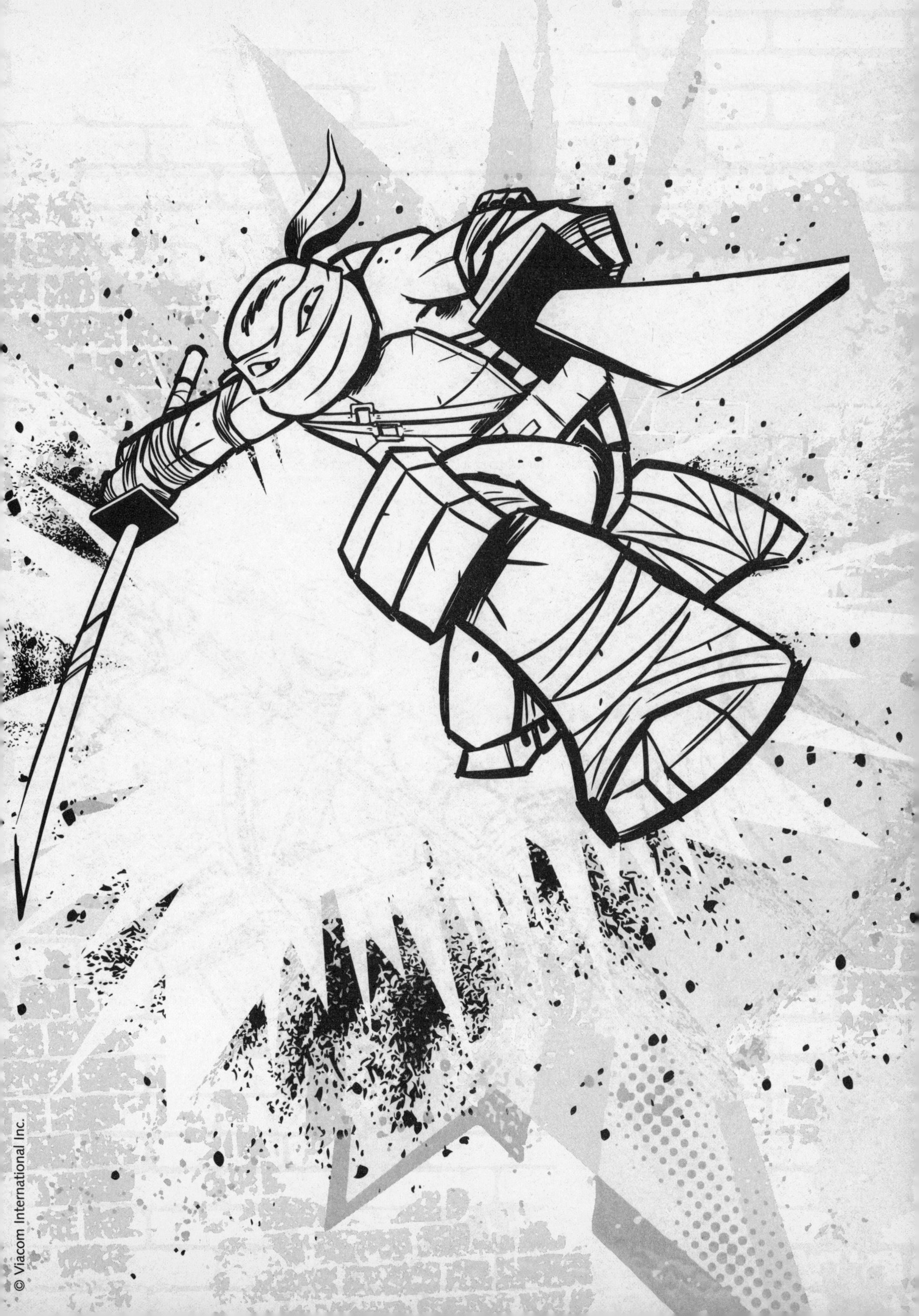

Raphael is ready for action!

Leo and Mikey slash and smash evil!

Raph and Donnie are on the hunt
for bad guys—and pizza!

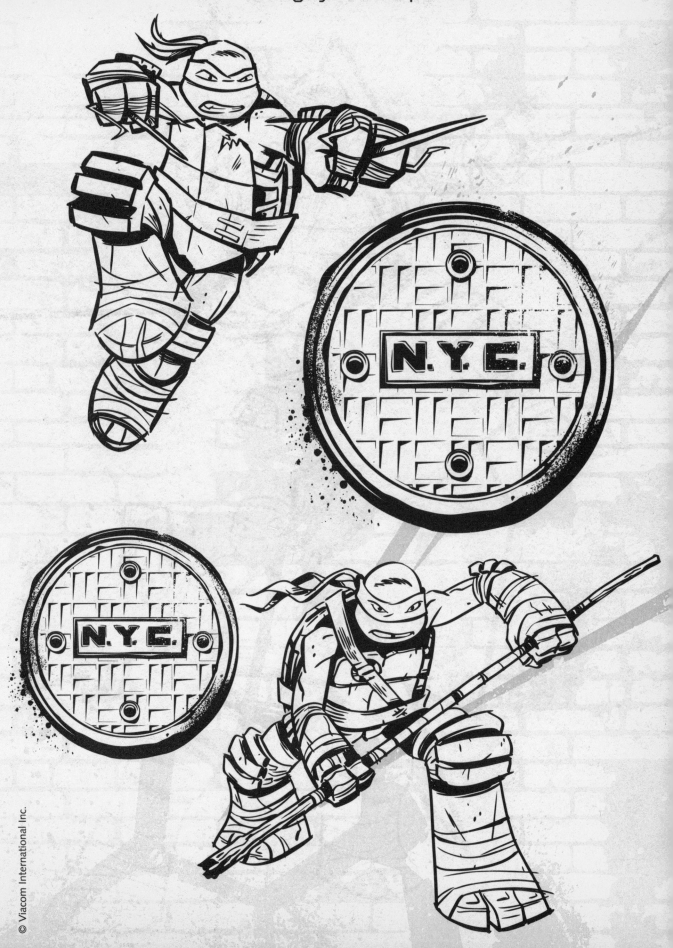

Donatello and Leonardo are
an awesome duo!

Turtle team-up!

We are heroes!

It's time to chill with the Turtles!

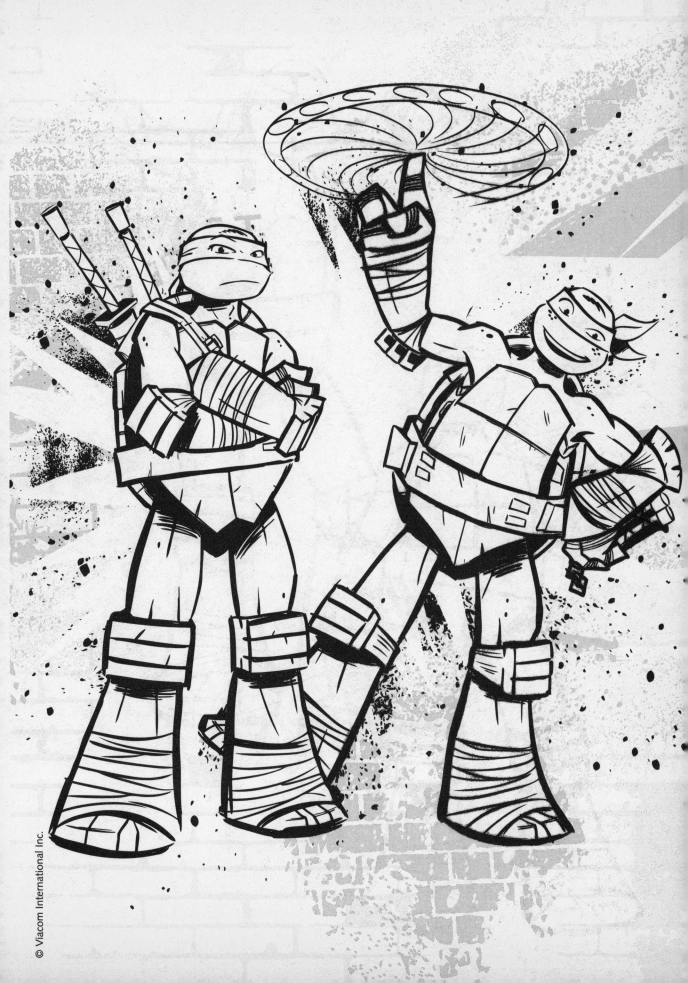

Unstoppable!

Go green!

Leonardo is the leader
of the group.

Donatello battles with his *bo* staff.

Raphael rarely misses his mark.

Mikey makes bad guys wish
they'd never met him.

Bad Guys, Beware!

Donatello makes fighting crime
look easy!

Turtle Power!

How many times can you find the word NINJA in the puzzle?

Look up, down, forward, backward, and diagonally.

A A N N I N J A A
A J N I N I J N J
N N A N N J N I N
I I N J A J A N I
N N I A N I A J N

ANSWER: 6.

Circle the picture of Leonardo that is different.

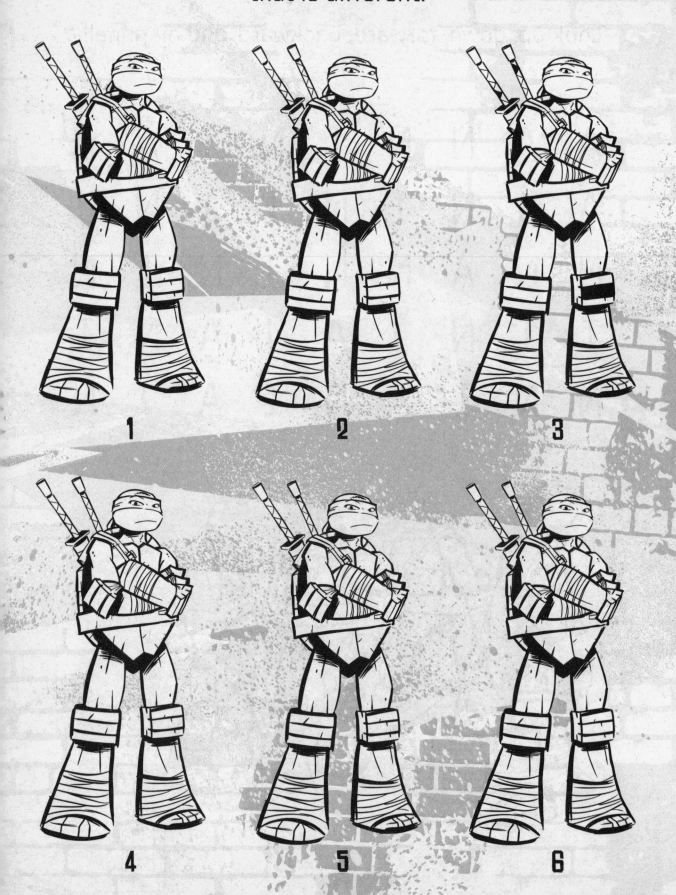

1

2

3

4

5

6

Leonardo loves to practice *ninjutsu.*

Michelangelo thinks he's
the funniest brother!

Solve the maze to help Michelangelo find Leonardo.

START

FINISH

Raphael is ready for anything!

What is the name of the swords Leonardo uses?

To find out, follow the lines and write each letter in the correct box.

A T K A A N

Raphael fights first—and asks
questions later!

Raphael's weapons of choice
are daggers called *sais*!

Color only the stars that have
the letters in Raphael's name.

ANSWER:

A martial arts teacher is called a sensei.

To find out the name of the Turtles' sensei,
follow the lines and write each letter
in the correct box.

N P R I E T S L

Circle the two pictures of Donatello that are exactly the same.

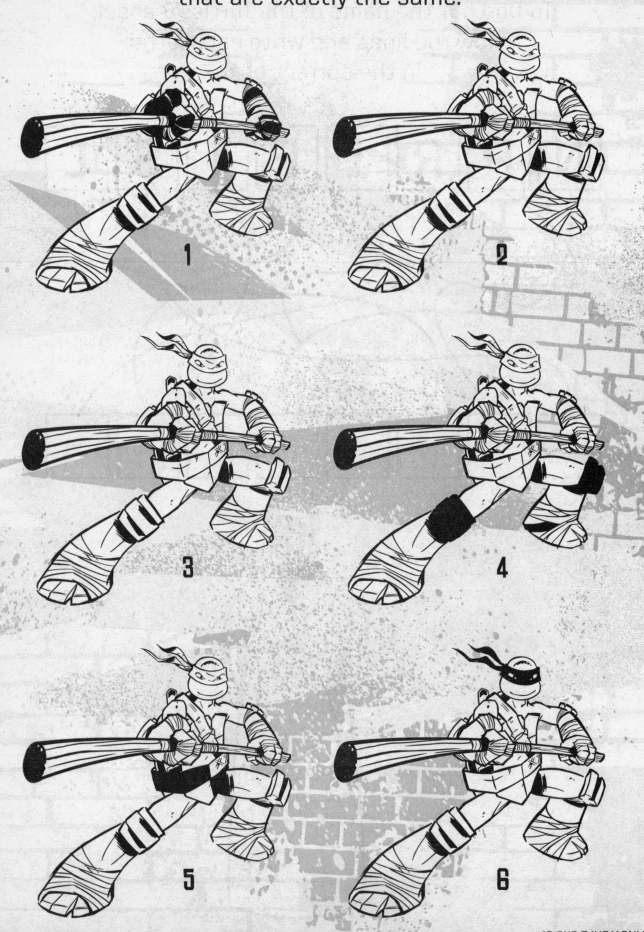

1

2

3

4

5

6

Donnie is the brains
of the group.

What does Donnie like to do?

To find out, replace each letter below with the one that comes before it in the alphabet.

I F J O W F O U T

__ _____

H B E H F U T U P

_____ __

L F F Q I J T

____ ___

C S P U I F S T T B G F

_____ ____!

Circle the shadow that belongs to Raphael.

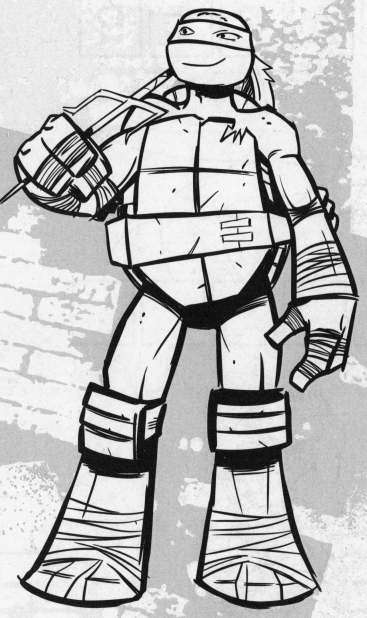

A

B

C

D

ANSWER: D.

What is the name of the weapon Donatello uses?

To find out, follow the lines and write each letter in the correct box.

F	O	S	A	F	T	B

Ninjas-in-training!

Help Mikey track down this villain by solving the maze.

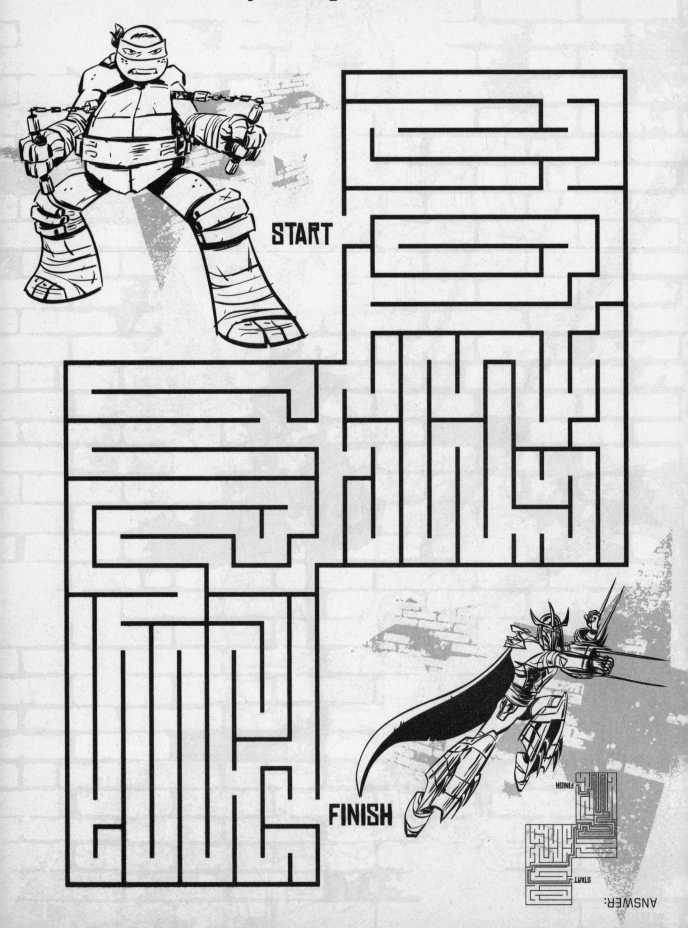

START

FINISH

ANSWER:

To find out the name of this villain, cross out every T.
Then write the remaining letters in order
on the blanks.

T S T T H T R T E

T T D D T E T R

_ _ _ _ _ _ _ _ _

Shredder takes on the Turtles!

Draw a line from each Ninja Turtle to his close-up.

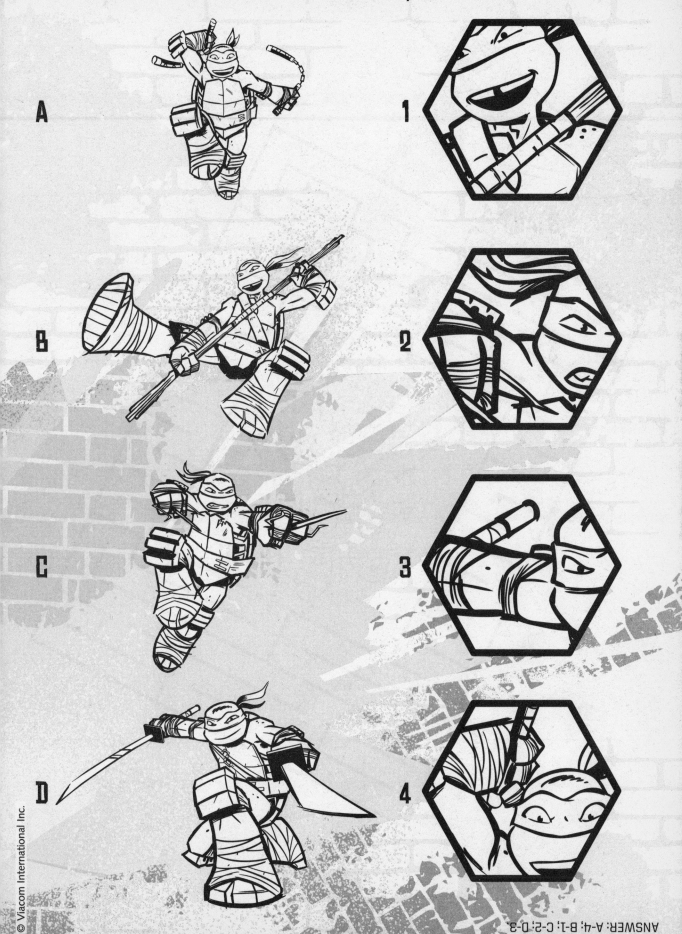

A

B

C

D

1

2

3

4

ANSWER: A-4, B-1, C-2, D-3.

Help Splinter find the Turtles
by solving the maze.

START

FINISH

Raphael is the rebel of the group.

What is the name of the weapon
Michelangelo uses?

To find out, follow the lines and write each letter
in the correct box.

K N U C H S U N C

TEENAGE MUTANT NINJA TURTLES™

HALF-SHELL HEROES!

Deep underground in the sewers live the Teenage Mutant Ninja Turtles, who train under Master Splinter.

The Turtles must work hard
to master their ninja skills.

Wham! The Turtles cannot defend against Splinter's surprise attack.

The Turtles need a break!

Can you spot the turtle shell that is different from the others?

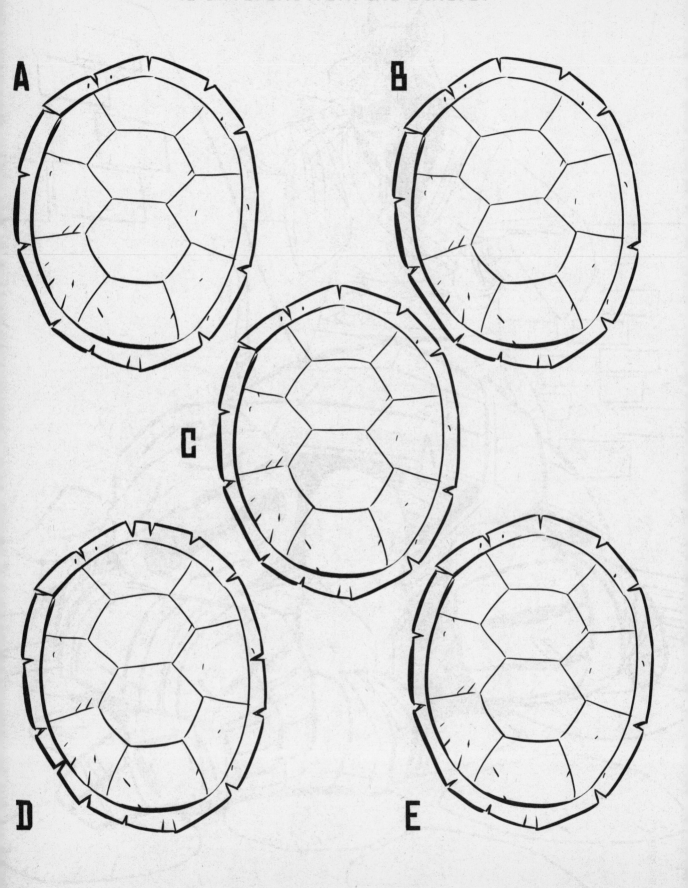

A

B

C

D

E

Leonardo is the brave leader of the Turtles.

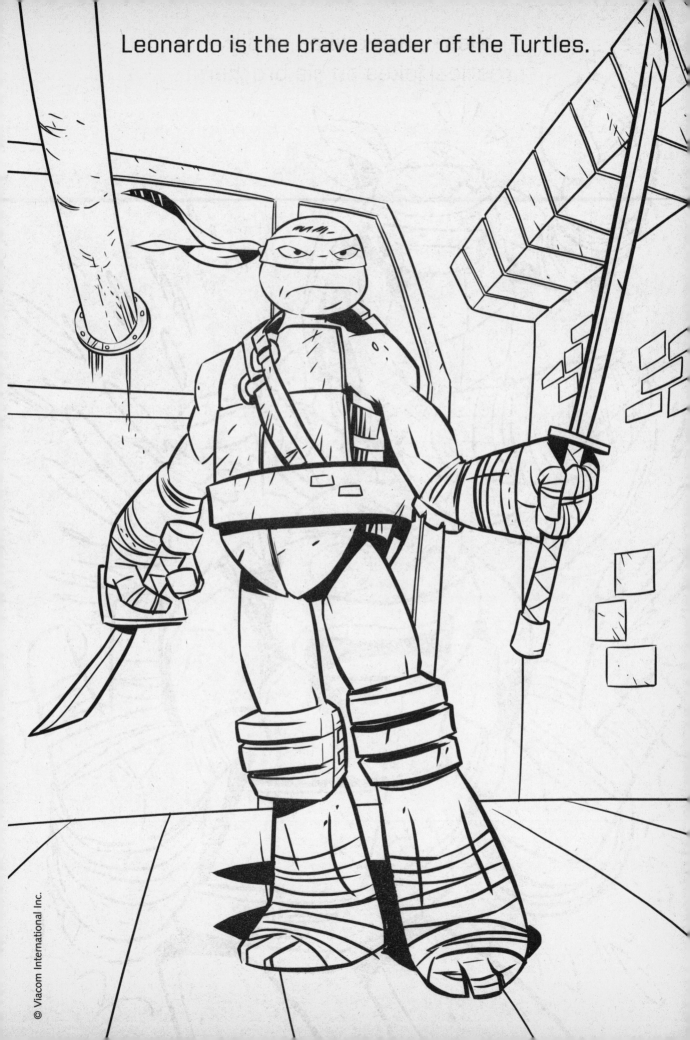

Michelangelo likes to play
practical jokes on his brothers!

Raphael doesn't think
Mikey's jokes are very funny.

In his secret science lab, Donatello builds the Turtles a new Patrol Buggy.

The Turtles fear that Shredder
is planning his next attack.

April is on a mission to
help her friends the Turtles.

She discovers that the Purple
Dragons are plotting against the Turtles!

April delivers a pizza to the Purple Dragons. Little do they know that the pizza contains a hidden microphone!

The Turtles listen in on the Purple Dragons
as they discuss Shredder's evil plan.

"Our home is no longer safe," Splinter says.
"Shredder must be stopped."

The Turtles each wear a different mask.
Decorate your own ninja mask below!

While tracking down the Purple Dragons, the Turtles run into the giant mutant Dogpound!

The Turtles are no match for Dogpound.
They must retreat!

Leo tosses a smoke bomb.

Color the smoke to help the
Turtles escape from Dogpound!

The Turtles are unhappy that they had to retreat from Dogpound.

"We need to find out how Shredder plans to attack your home," says April. "And I'm the only one who can do it."

April spies on the Foot Clan hideout and overhears their evil plot.

Shredder is planning to steal a tanker filled with a dangerous chemical!

The Turtles' home will be destroyed if Shredder pours the chemical into the sewer system!

April follows Shredder's
henchmen, but they spot her!

Dogpound captures April and locks her in the Foot Clan's van.

The Turtles zoom to the rescue
in their new Patrol Buggy.

The tanker filled with a dangerous chemical arrives on the scene.

Dogpound rips open the tanker door and takes the driver's seat.

The Turtles will need to split up if they want to save April *and* stop Shredder!

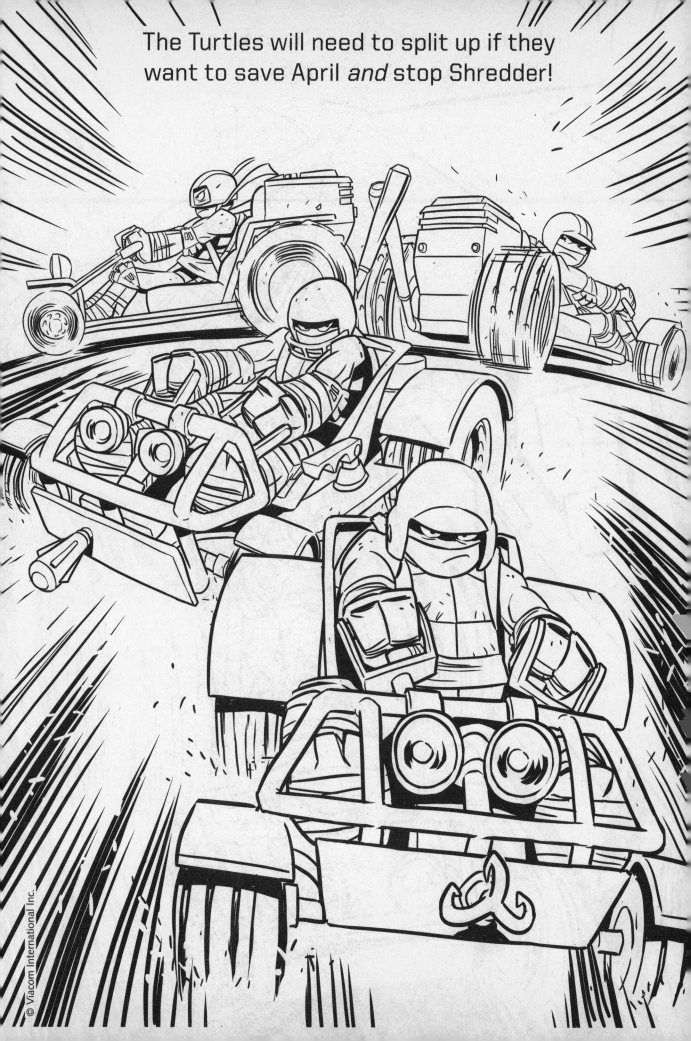

"Hold your breath, April!" Donnie calls as he throws a smoke bomb into the van.

Help Mikey and Leo get to the tanker before Dogpound can carry out Shredder's evil plot!

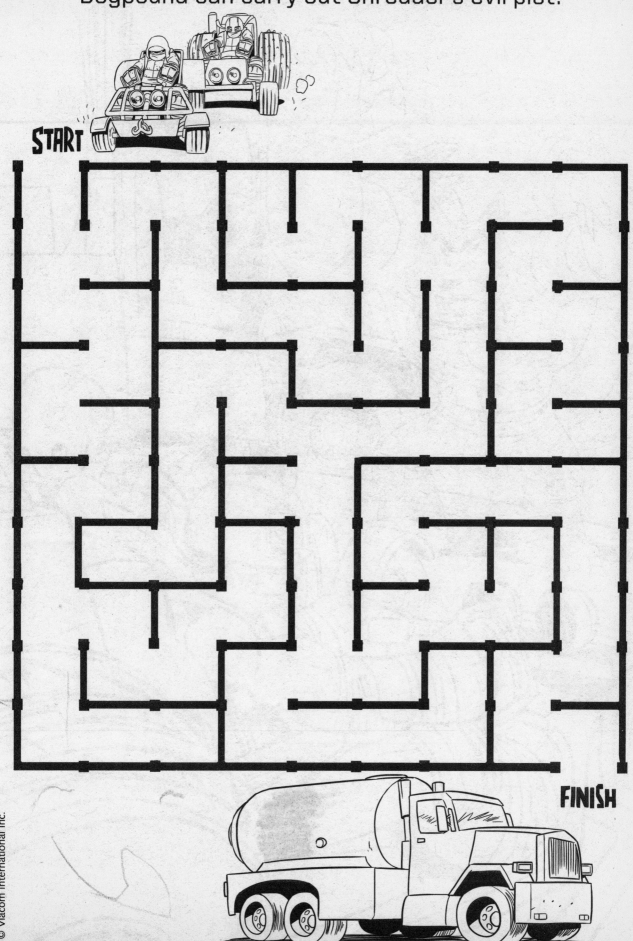

START

FINISH

Mikey and Leo follow
Dogpound to the stolen tanker.

Look out! Dogpound rips the cover off
a manhole and throws it at the Turtles.

Mikey and Leo draw their weapons and prepare to fight.

Leo's sword cuts open the tanker's side, and the chemical spills onto the street.

Leo has an idea. "Mikey, throw your water balloon at the acid!"

The water reacts with the acid, causing the tanker to explode!

"Nothing says victory like the sweet taste of pizza!"

Help the Turtles celebrate by
drawing some toppings on the pizza.

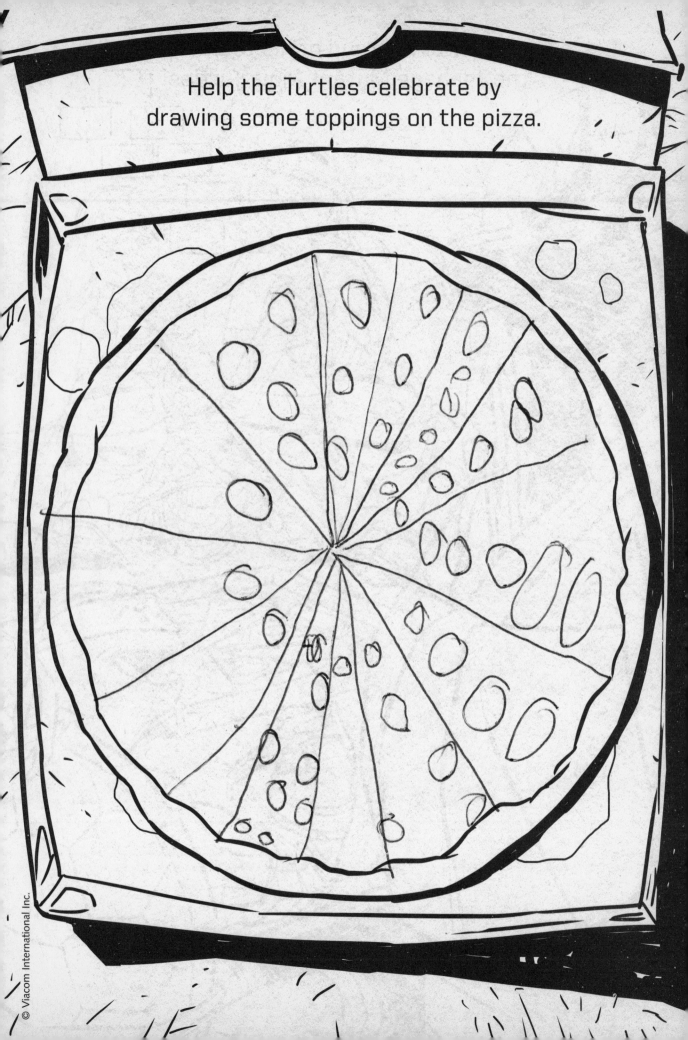

Splinter is proud of his team—
the Teenage Mutant Ninja Turtles!

TEENAGE MUTANT NINJA TURTLES™

MUTANTS RULE!

Color the picture of Michelangelo that is different.

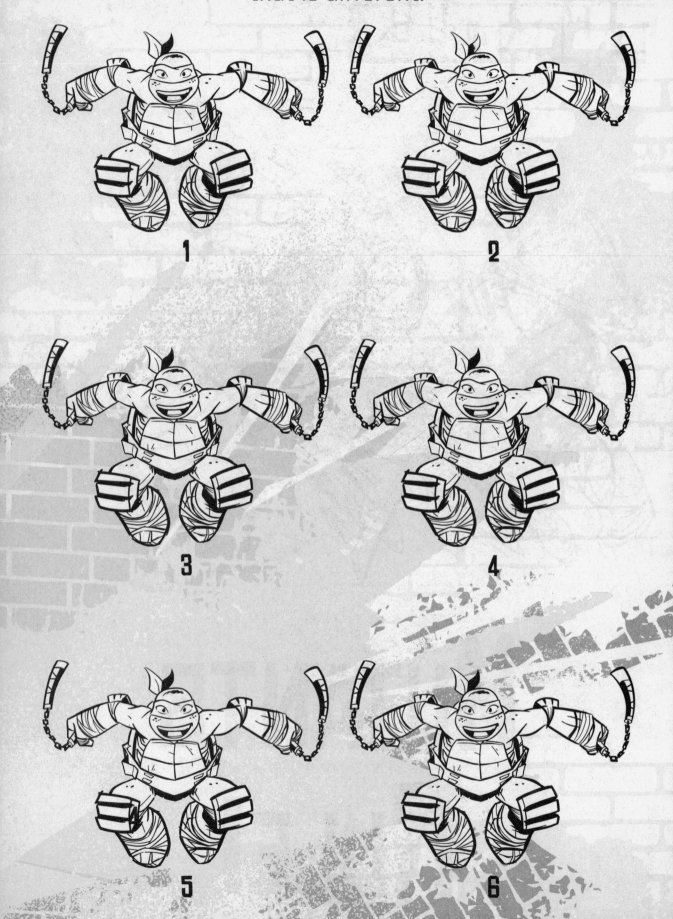

1

2

3

4

5

6

Solve the maze to help Raphael find Donatello.

START

FINISH

ANSWER:

Leonardo is a fierce fighting machine!

Shredder is the leader of a secret group of ninjas.

To find out its name, cross out every Z.
Then write the remaining letters in order on the blanks.

ZTZHZZEZEZFZZOZ

OZZTZZCZLZAZN

_ _ _ _ _ _ _ _ _ _ _ _ _

The Foot Clan attacks!

How many soldiers can you count?

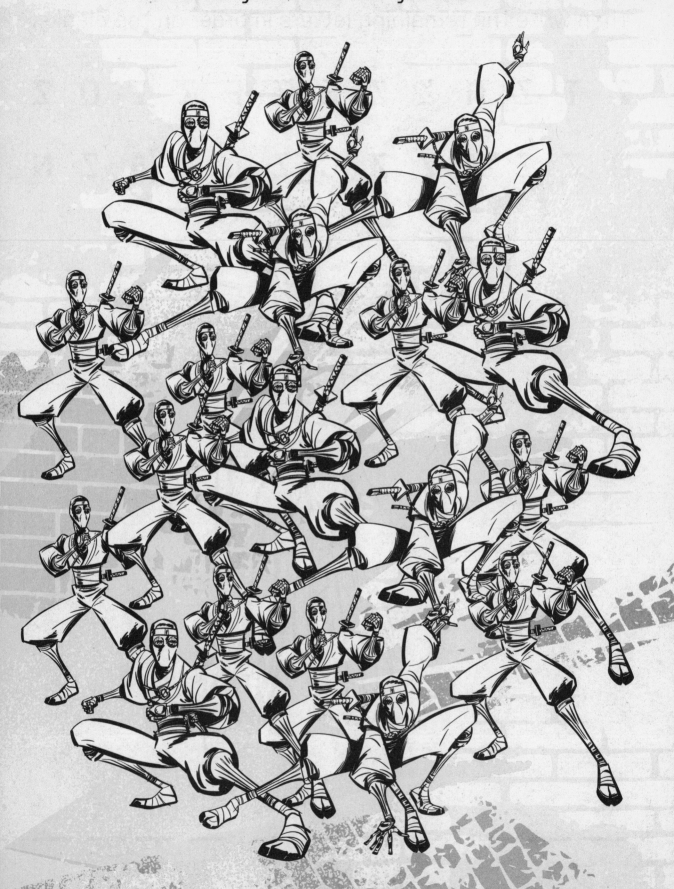

Let the battle begin!

Find the line that leads Donatello to these Foot Clan soldiers.

START

A B C

FINISH

Complete the bottom picture by drawing Leonardo's *katana* sword.

Use the key to learn the name of the evil organization that controls these robots.

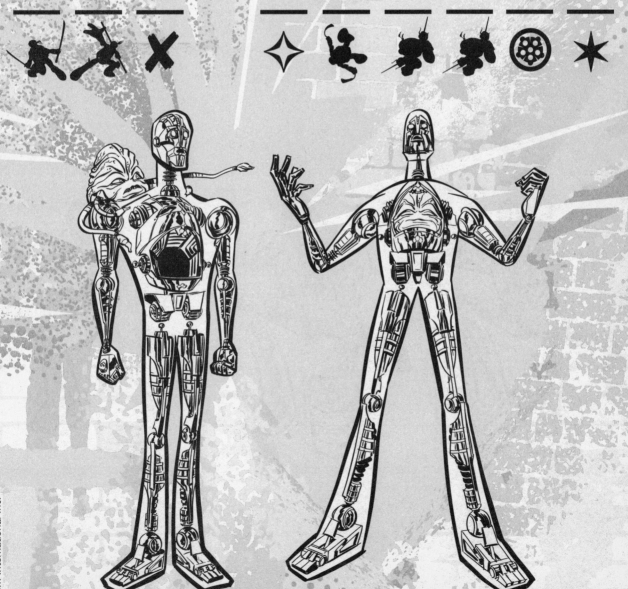

Circle the picture that is different.

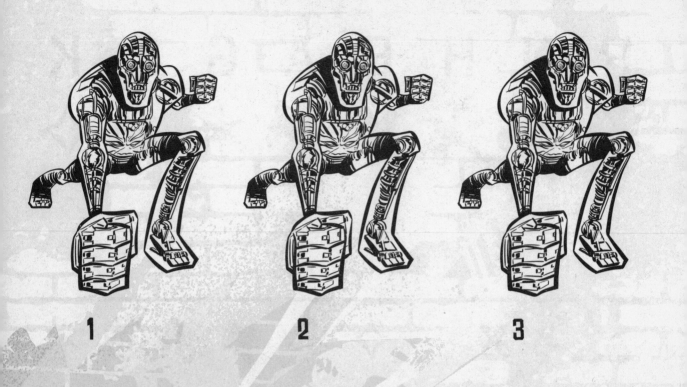

1   2   3

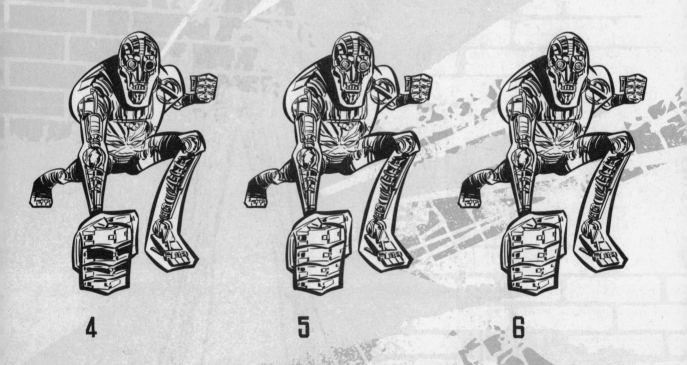

4   5   6

The Kraang are a race of aliens!

Solve the maze to help the Ninja Turtles stop the Kraang!

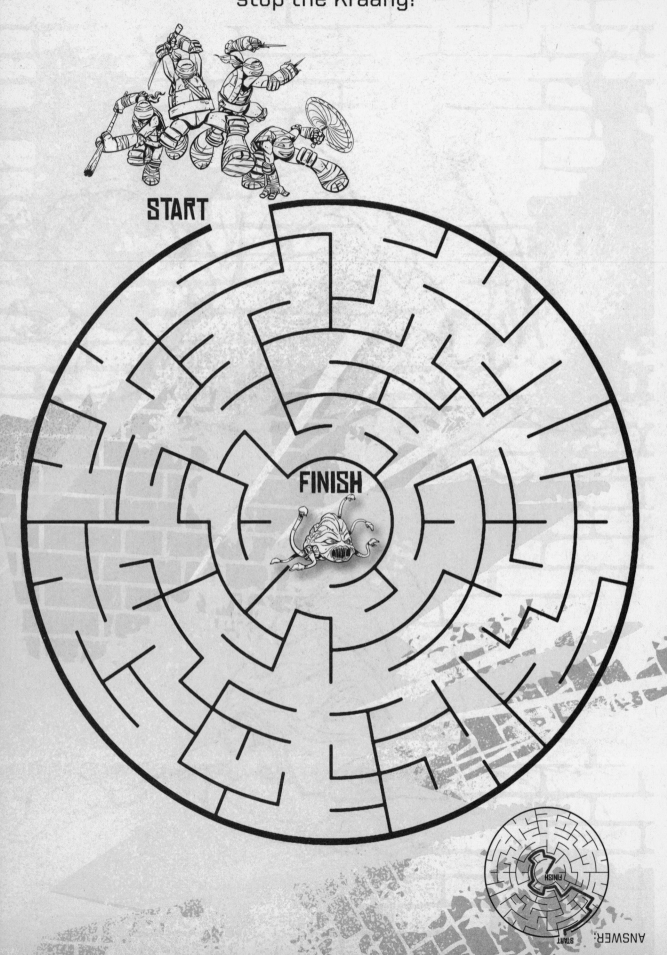

START

FINISH

What happened to April's father?

To find out, start at the arrow and, going clockwise
around the circle, write the letters in order
on the blanks below.

_ _ _ _ _ _ _ _ _ _ _ _

_ _ _ _ _ _ _ _ _ _ _ _

_ _ _ _ _ _ _ _ _ _ _ !

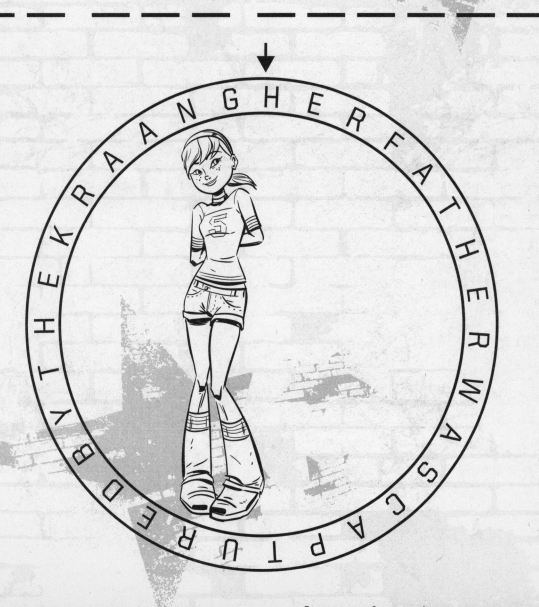

ANSWER: Her father was captured by the Kraang!

In each row, circle the picture that is different.

The Teenage Mutant Ninja Turtles team up
to take down Shredder!

Color this Teenage Mutant Ninja Turtles poster!

Help Leonardo find the path that leads to his brothers.

START

A B C

FINISH

Circle the shadow that belongs to Shredder.

A

B

C

D

Color this poster of Michelangelo.

Mikey wipes out!

Color this poster of Raphael.

Raphael is sharp!

Color this poster of Leonardo.

Leonardo slices and dices!

Color this poster of Donatello.

Donatello battles the Foot Clan!

Donatello takes a break . . . for pizza!

Leonardo and Michelangelo smell pizza.

Solve the maze to help them find Donatello and Raphael.

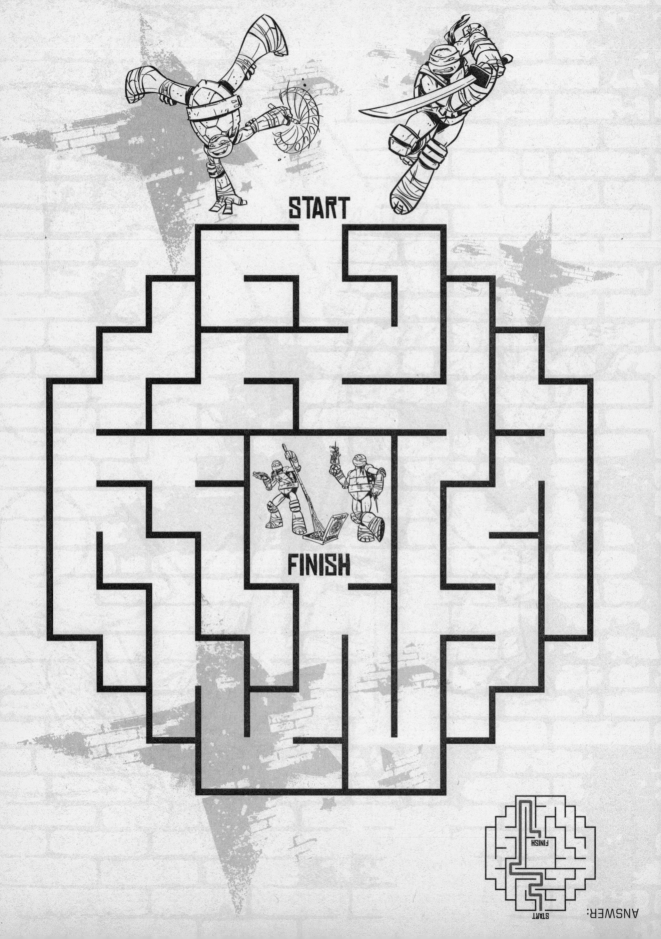

START

FINISH

How many times can you find the word TURTLE in the puzzle?

Look up, down, forward, backward, and diagonally.

```
T U R T T T E
E L T R U T L
E T U R R E T
L E T U T L R
T L E T L L R
E R U T E R T
T U R T L E E
```

ANSWER: 5.

Draw a line from each Foot Clan soldier to his close-up.

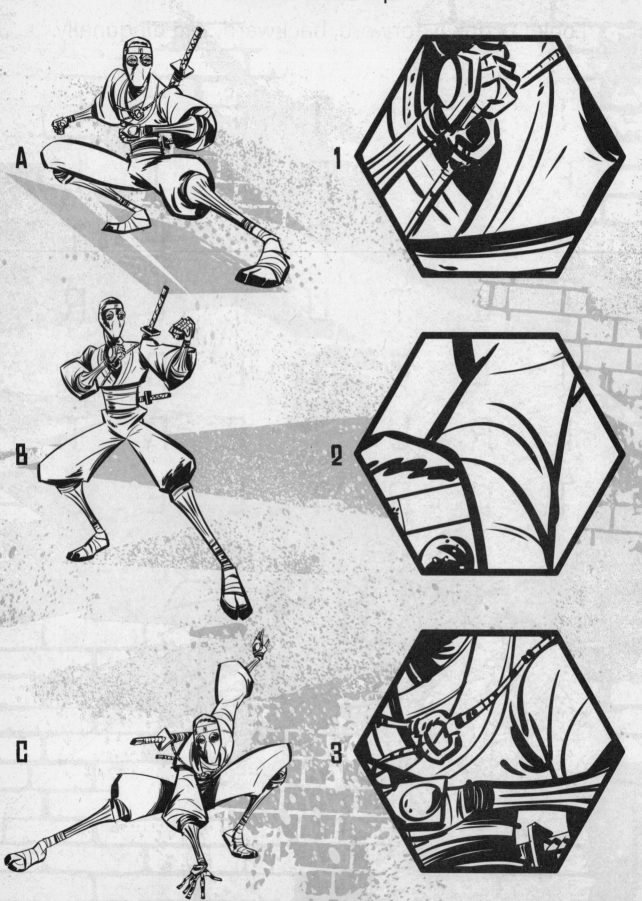

Color this action-packed poster!

The Turtles save the day!

TEENAGE MUTANT NINJA TURTLES

THE ART OF THE NINJA!

The Turtles each wear a mask.

Draw three more for them.

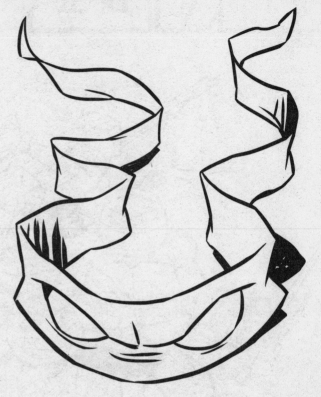

Draw a mask on Leo.

Leonardo leads with steel.

Finish his sword.

Draw a mask on Raphael.

Help Raph make a point!

Finish his *sais*.

Draw a mask on Donatello.

Donnie battles with his *bo* staff!

Draw a mask on Michelangelo.

Give Mikey some flying *nunchucks*.

Finish the picture of Michelangelo.

Who hit Raphael with a water balloon?

Watch out! Raphael is really angry.
Draw some steam and lightning over his head.

Donnie's built a robot called Metalhead.

Invent your own robot!

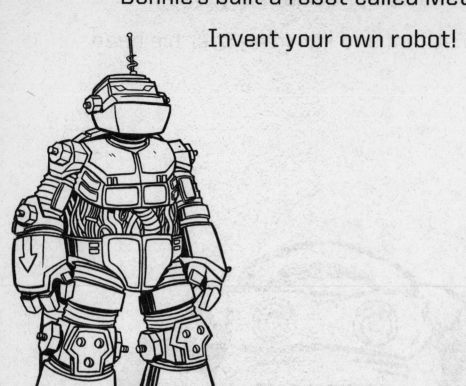

Who is Metalhead fighting?

Leo and Mikey are ready to spar—
but where are their weapons?

Finish the picture of Leonardo.

Did someone call for a pizza?

Draw a pizza box balanced on Mikey's finger.

Time to celebrate.
Draw some more pizza for the other Turtles.

April is doing some spy work.

What does she see?

Donnie rushes to help April.

What is he jumping over?

Draw a Kraang in this droid.

Finish the picture and get Donnie
ready for his next adventure.

BLAAM! What is the Kraang-droid blasting?

Here come the Kraang!

Finish building the Kraang-droid.

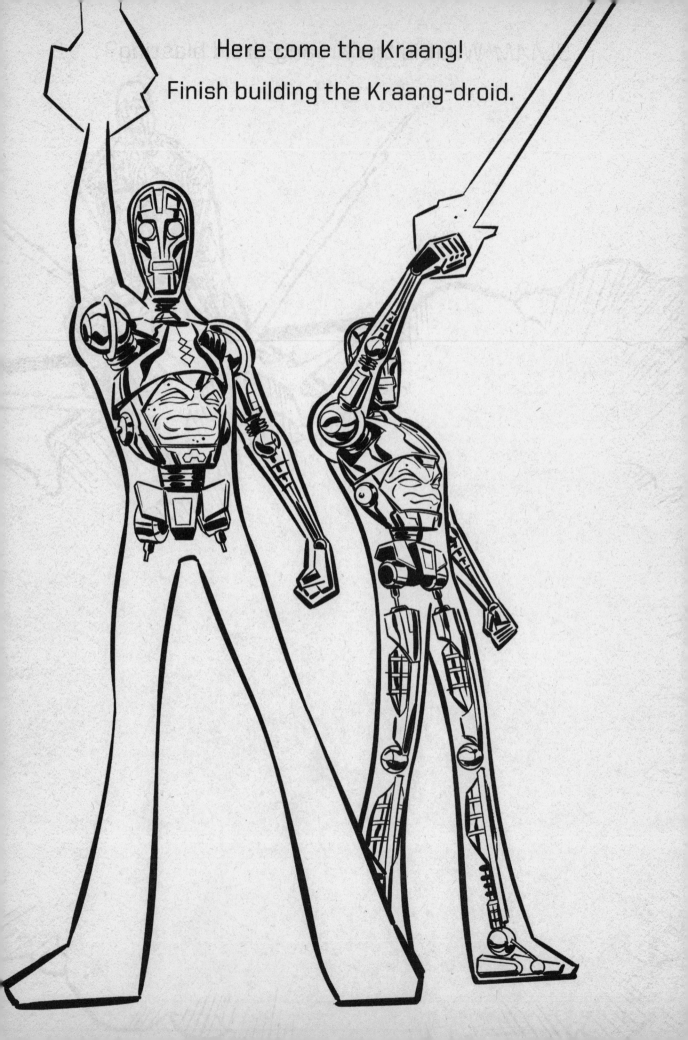

Who is Leo about to battle?

The Turtles are ready for battle.
Who's coming down the sewer tunnel?

Draw something for Dogpound to smash!

Draw some robotic legs for Fishface.

It's a good night for a fight.
Draw New York City behind Leo and Raph.

Who's got Donnie's back?

Time to hit the streets!
Draw Leo in his buggy behind Mikey.

What are the Turtles hiding from?

Prepare Shredder for battle.
Draw some big blades on his glove.

Who will stop Shredder?

Copy the top picture onto the bottom grid.